This book is
PANTS!

JOHN KANE

D0184880

RULE 1

ALWAYS
WEAR
PANTS

RULE 2

ALWAYS WEAR
THE RIGHT
PANTS

TO THE READER

EVERY TIME YOU SEE A
PAIR OF **PANTS** IN THIS BOOK,
HOLD THEM UP IN FRONT
OF YOU LIKE THIS.

It all started one day when I decided to go to space.
I built a rocket and made a helmet.
But something was missing.

I needed

SPACE PANTS

When I reached the moon, I met an alien called Buzzly.

He spoke a strange language.

I had to understand it, and quickly.

This called for some

SMARTY PANTS

Now I understood:
Buzzly wanted to visit Earth.
Mmm, I thought.
An alien on Earth might be a problem . . .

unless we wore
BEACH
PANTS

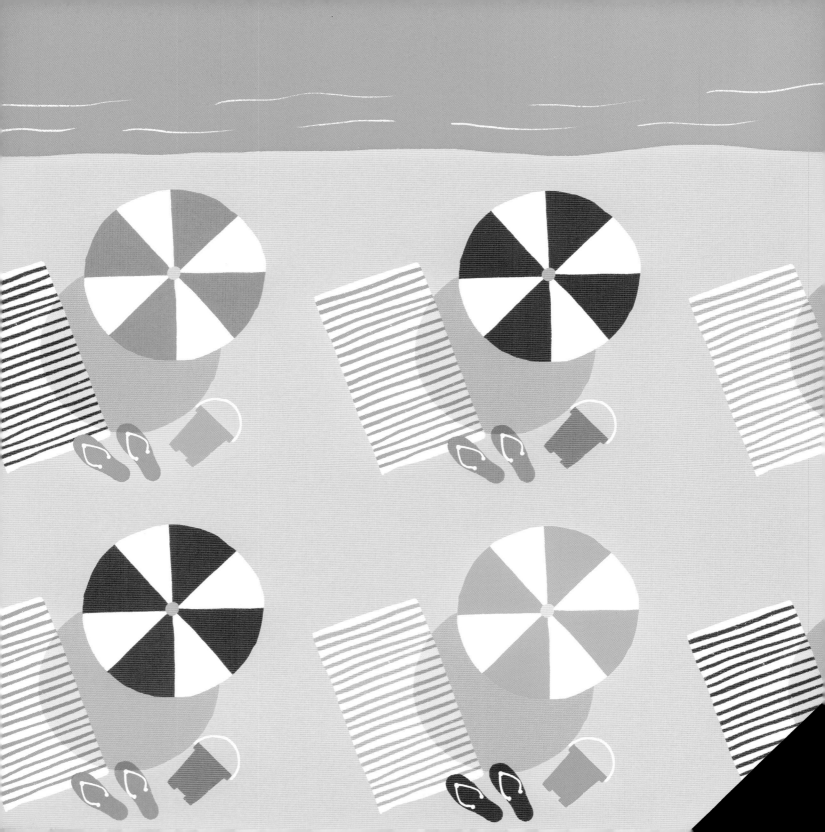

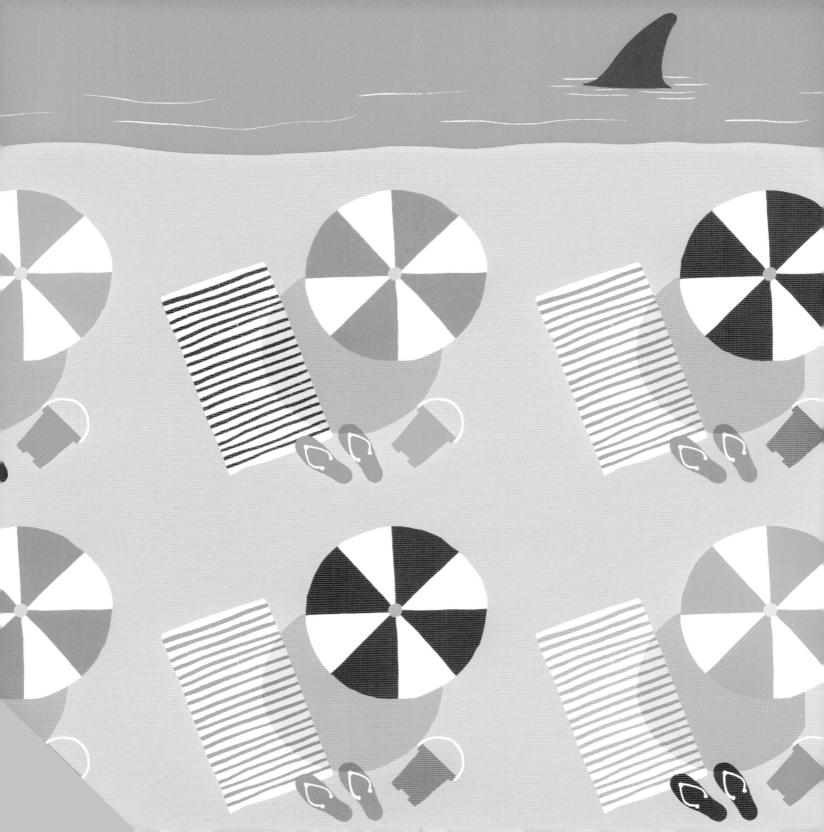

As soon as we landed, everyone started freaking out,
even though Buzzly was being really friendly.
We needed to get out of there.

We needed

SPEEDY PANTS

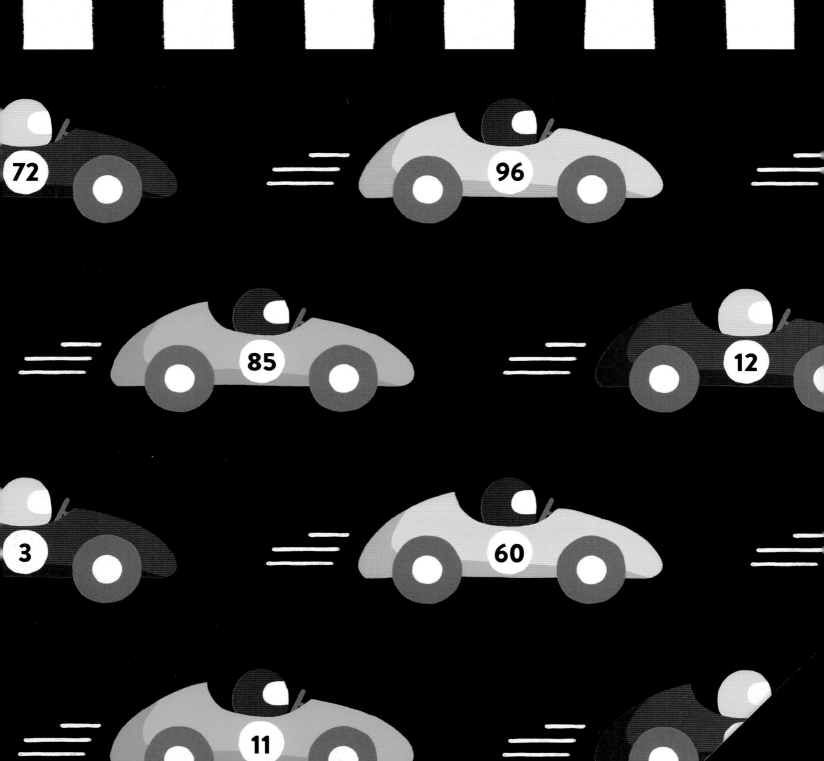

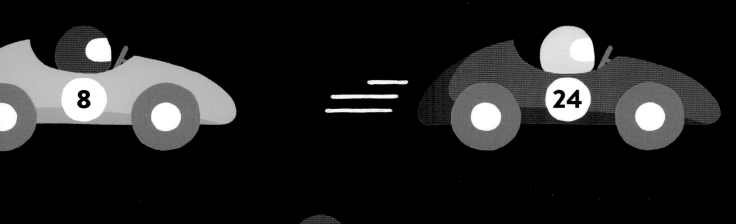
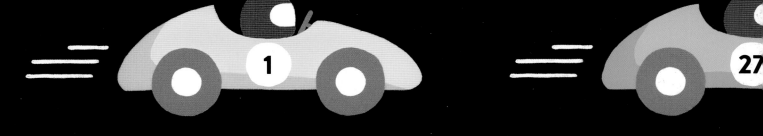

The speedy pants made us super fast,
but by now everyone on Earth was looking for us.
We had to climb up into the trees.

And the best way to climb is in . . .

MONKEY PANTS

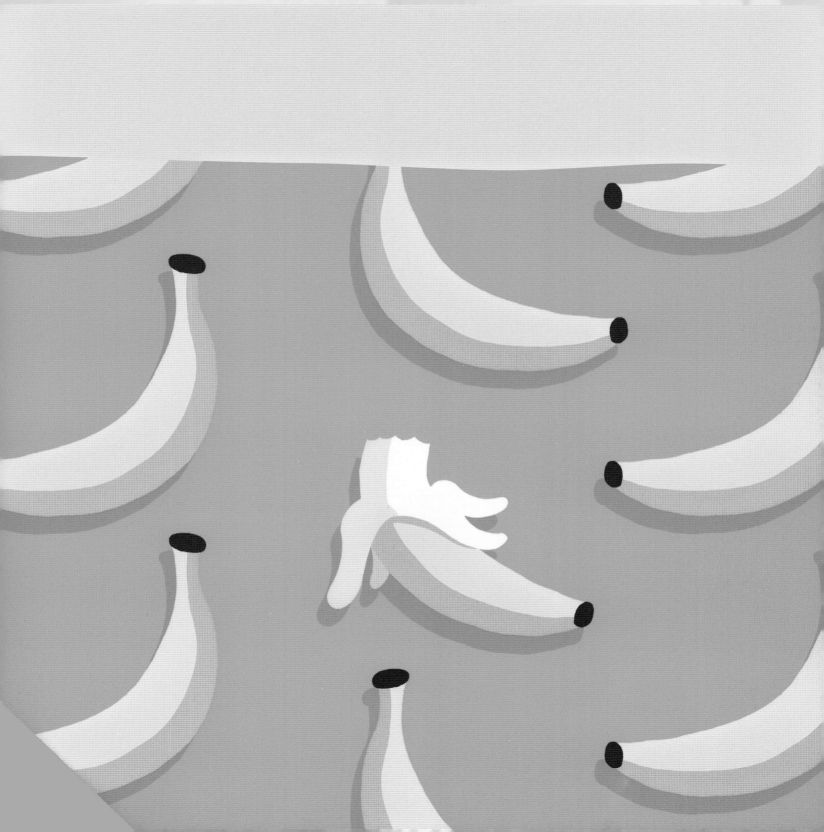

PHEW!

We were safe.

Until it got dark and Buzzly was soooo scared.
We needed to get out of the forest.

Time for
BRIGHT
PANTS

Now we could see. But we were freezing cold,
and it was only getting colder.

We needed

HOT PANTS

They kept us toasty warm. By now we were really
hungry though. I asked Buzzly what he liked to eat.
It was my favourite too.

So we ordered some,

and put on our

PIZZA
PANTS

While we were eating our pizza, all the people chasing us arrived. They weren't afraid – they just wanted to welcome Buzzly to our planet.

This called for a party.
And a party needs

PARTY PANTS

It was the best day ever.
And the best day ever
needs the
BEST
PANTS
EVER

It was time to go.

I had a new best friend
and we were ready for new adventures,
with new pants,
in new places.

Where do you think
we'll go next?

Also by John Kane:

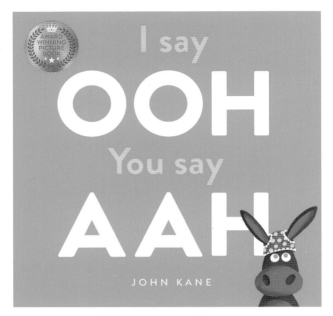

ISBN: 978-1-78370-872-7

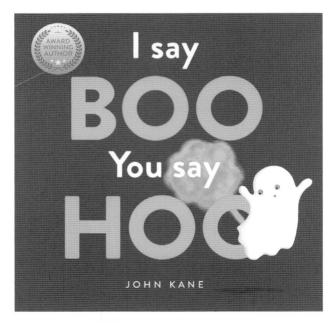

ISBN: 978-1-78741-550-8